Apple Tree Christmas

A HOLIDAY CLASSIC

Apple Tree Christmas

TRINKA HAKES NOBLE

My heartfelt thanks to Sleeping Bear Press
for reissuing *Apple Tree Christmas*.

Trinka

Text and Illustration Copyright © 1984 Trinka Hakes Noble
Text and Illustration Copyright © 2005 Trinka Hakes Noble

First published in 1984 by Dial Books for Young Readers
A Division of Penguin Putnam Books for Young Readers

Sleeping Bear Press

2395 South Huron Parkway, Ste. 200
Ann Arbor, MI 48104
www.sleepingbearpress.com

Printed and bound in the United States

10 9 8 7 6 5 4 3 2

Library of Congress Cataloging-in-Publication Data on file.
ISBN: 1-58536-270-0

For my wise and wonderful Father,

who made a drawing board for me,
many years ago...
on which I drew this book for him,
many years later...

In loving memory of my Father

Carl Martin Hakes

September 30, 1906 – September 30, 1999

The Ansterburgs lived in the end of an old barn. Underneath, Mrs. Wooly and her lambs softly moved about; Old Dan bumped in his stall; and Sweet Clover mooed at milking time. On the first floor Mama cooked on a big black stove and Papa worked in his woodshop, and above, Katrina and Josie slept in the hayloft. Someday Papa would build them a real house. But for now living in the barn with the soft animal sounds and sweet smell of hay was just right.

Near the barn was an old apple tree. It was overgrown with wild grape vines but Papa never cut away the vines because they made a natural ladder to the highest apples. "Besides," he always joked, "I could never separate such close friends."

"Girls, we'll be picking apples soon," said Mama one day. "Maybe sooner than you think," said Papa. "I heard they got a foot of snow up north."
"Oh, dear," fretted Mama, "winter so soon."
"We'd better get the apples in tomorrow," said Papa.
"And I'll make a big batch of apple butter," said Mama. "You girls should stay home from school to help sort apples."

"Hurray!" shouted Katrina and Josie.

The next morning the ground was white, but even in the snow sorting apples was fun. Some went into a pile for cider and applesauce, some went into baskets for pies, small ones were for their lunch pails, and the bruised ones were for Old Dan. But finding the apples to decorate their Christmas tree was what Katrina and Josie liked the best. All day long they picked and chose until the most beautiful apples of all stood on the stone wall. Then Mama picked the biggest one.

"This will make a nice clove apple for our Christmas dinner table," she said. They wrapped the rest of the apples in cloth and Papa put them in the bottom of the barn to keep until Christmas.

Now that all the apples were picked, Katrina and Josie could climb the tree as much as they wanted. The snowy weather didn't stop them. Every day after school they would play in its branches.

On one side Papa had pulled a thick vine down low enough to make a swing for Josie.

The other side of the tree belonged to Katrina. One limb made a perfect drawing board. She called it her studio. There she would dream and draw until the cold winter sun glowed low behind the trees.

"Time for chores," called Mama as she lit the lantern.

Katrina and Josie ran inside the barn and climbed down the
ladder to the animals' stalls. First they shelled corn for the
hens, then they fed and watered Old Dan. They saved Mrs.
Wooly and her family until last so they could stick their cold
fingers deep into her wool coat.

"How warm you are, Mrs. Wooly," said Katrina.

"Just as warm as the scarf and socks we're knitting for Papa's Christmas presents, right, Katrina?" asked Josie.

"Shhh! He might hear you," scolded Katrina.

But Papa didn't hear them. He was busy putting Mrs. Wooly and her family in with Old Dan and Sweet Clover.

"Papa, what are you doing?" asked Katrina.

"We'll put the stock together tonight so they can keep warm. You climb up and stuff straw in those holes. It must have dropped twenty degrees in the last hour," said Papa.

"Do you think we're in for a blizzard?" asked Katrina.

"Wouldn't be a bit surprised. Probably be forty below by morning."

Katrina could feel the north wind blowing through the holes in the barn. Papa spread a thick layer of straw around the animals. Then he watered them again because by morning their trough would be frozen solid.

It was cold upstairs, too, but Mama had moved the table close to the stove and a hot supper of apple fritters and maple syrup soon warmed them up.

That night the blizzard hit with full force. The old barn shook
and its beams creaked as if they were in pain.

In the loft Katrina woke with a start. She could hear Papa and
Mama talking softly below. "Probably be gone by morning," Papa
said. So she snuggled closer to Josie and went back to sleep.

But the blizzard got worse and lasted for three days and nights.

On the third night something strange woke Katrina. The wind was howling and the beams were screaming but there was a different sound, one more frightening—like a million sharp knives slashing the roof, cutting the barn, trying to get in.

Katrina was so frightened that she started to scream but Mama and Papa were already there wrapping them up in quilts.

"Papa, what is it?" asked Katrina, shaking with fright.
"Ice storm. We're moving you girls downstairs in case the roof caves in under the weight."

Mama put Katrina and Josie on a featherbed under the table. "Now try to sleep," she said.

But Katrina couldn't fall asleep. The ice storm tore at the barn and throughout the night Katrina was startled by the loud splintering sounds of big limbs snapping like twigs.

When Mama opened the stove door to add more wood, the firelight made an eerie orange glow. Her shadow looked big and strange. Katrina knew Mama would keep the fire going, no matter what.

The next morning there was calm. The storm had passed. Katrina was glad until she saw Papa's long face when he came inside.

"Ice storm took the old apple tree," he said.
"But surely the vines would hold it together," said Mama.
"No, it split right down through the middle. I'll chop it up for firewood," said Papa.

Katrina ran to the window and knelt down. Through her tears she saw nothing but a heap of snow and ice and dead branches.

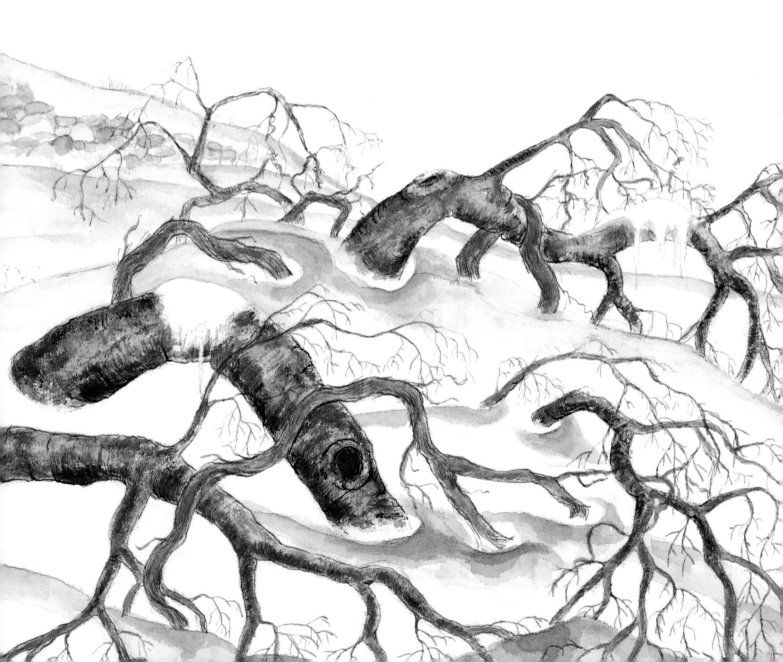

Every morning Papa brought in another pile of firewood and vines from the apple tree. Mama said they should keep busy knitting Papa's Christmas presents. Josie finished Papa's scarf and made one for Mama, too. Katrina worked on Mama's pin-cushion, but she just couldn't concentrate on knitting Papa's socks while he sawed and hacked away at the apple tree. She had ripped out the heel and started over so many times that she had all but ruined the yarn from Mrs. Wooly.

"Well, I'll miss the old apple tree," said Mama, "but it will keep us warm this long winter."
"Yes, I'm thankful for the firewood," said Papa.

How could he be thankful, thought Katrina. *Didn't he know that he was chopping up her studio? Didn't he know he was ruining her drawing board? Didn't he know she couldn't draw unless she were in the apple tree?*

The day before Christmas came. Mama made her clove apple and began baking pies. Papa brought in a fresh pine tree and they decorated it with the beautiful apples. But to Katrina it just didn't feel like Christmas.

Even when she went to bed on Christmas Eve, Papa was still sawing away at the apple tree.

On Christmas morning their stockings were filled with oranges, wild hickory nuts, black walnuts, and peppermint sticks. Josie gave Papa and Mama their scarves, and Katrina gave Mama the pincushion. But it still didn't feel like Christmas to Katrina.

Then Papa said, "Now my little ones, turn around and close your eyes. No peeking."

First Katrina heard Papa ask Mama to help him. Then she heard him hammering something to the beam, then he dragged something across the floor.

"All right, you can look now," said Mama.

They whirled around.

There, hanging from the beam, was Josie's swing, the very same vine swing from the apple tree. Sitting on the swing was a little rag doll that Mama had made.

Near the tree was a drawing board made from the very same limb that had been Katrina's studio. On the drawing board were real charcoal paper and three sticks of willow charcoal.

Katrina softly touched the drawing board. She wanted to say,
How wise and wonderful you are, Papa and *Thank you, Papa* and *I'll always love you, Papa.* But all she could say was, "Oh, Papa."

Papa didn't say anything either. He just handed her the three sticks of charcoal.

Josie began to swing with her doll and Katrina started to draw. Now she could see how beautiful Mama's clove apple looked on the white tablecloth and how shiny red the apples were on the Christmas tree. Now she could smell the fresh winter pine tree and the warm apple pies. Now it felt like Christmas.

Katrina gave her first drawing to Papa. It was a picture of the day when Papa picked the apples and Mama made apple butter and Katrina and Josie sorted the apples.

In the corner Papa wrote:

*This picture was drawn
by Katrina Ansterburg
on Christmas Day
1881.*

Then he hung it in his woodshop
and there it stayed for many long years.